Star Island

Star Island

Amy Tree

Illustrated by Gwen Millward

Orion
Children's Books

First published in Great Britain in 2009
by Orion Children's Books
a division of the Orion Publishing Group Ltd
Orion House
5 Upper St Martin's Lane
London WC2H 9EA
An Hachette UK Company

1 3 5 7 9 8 6 4 2

The Orion Publishing Group's policy is to use papers
that are natural, renewable and recyclable products and
made from wood grown in sustainable forests. The logging
and manufacturing processes are expected to conform to
the environmental regulations of the country of origin.

A catalogue record for this book is
available from the British Library.

ISBN: 978 1 84255 658 0

Printed and bound in the UK by
CPI Mackays, Chatham ME5 8TD

www.orionbooks.co.uk

For Gwen Millward – with thanks and appreciation

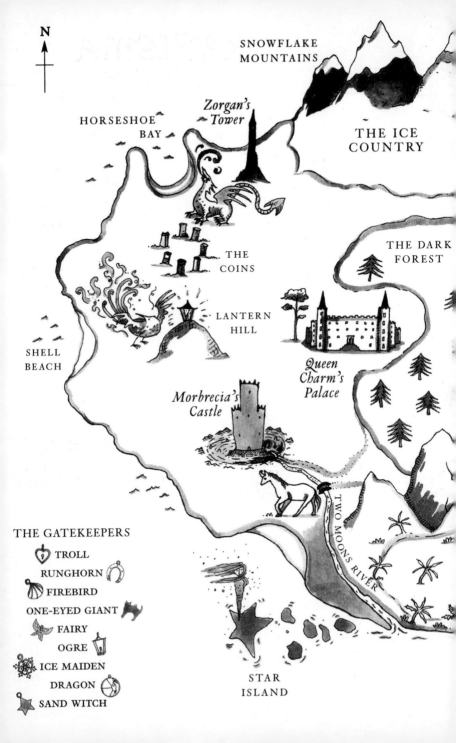

KARISMA

The Thirteen Charms of Karisma

When Charm became queen of Karisma, the wise and beautiful Silversmith made her a precious gift. It was a bracelet. On it were fastened thirteen silver amulets, which the Silversmith called 'charms', in honour of the new queen.

It was part of Karisma law. Whenever there was a new ruler the Silversmith made a special gift, to help them care for the world they had inherited. And this time it was a bracelet. She told Queen Charm it was magical because the charms held the power to control the forces of nature and keep everything in balance. She must take the greatest care of them. As long as she, and she alone, had possession of the charms all would be well.

And so it was, until the bracelet was stolen by a spider, and fell into the hands of Zorgan, the magician.

1

One

The Silversmith rolls the ancient parchment with care, winds a silver ribbon around it and ties it with a bow.

"A fascinating story," she muses, "and so vividly described by Silvesta.* To think, if it hadn't been for Sesame and her friends this important part of our history may never have been discovered!"

Placing the scroll in a drawer, the Silversmith locks it away. She feels honoured Queen Charm has entrusted her with the historic document.

"Silvesta's story explains everything about the origins of the Silver Pool," she remembers Charm saying. "Since you have charge of the magical silver it's only right you should look after it."

* * * * * * * * * * * * * * * * * * *
*Do you remember Silvesta's story? You can read it in Book Eight: *Secret Treasure*

3

Since then – since Charm's birthday about a mede✫ ago – she has read the story often, each time gaining more of an insight as to why the Silver Pool is so special. It's unique to Karisma and, of course, the charms she's created from this precious source are special too. Even *she* doesn't fully understand their power. Somehow their positive energy keeps everything in balance; together they keep nature under control – a force for good, protecting the fragile world in their care. As these thoughts race through her head, words from a familiar song dance off her lips:

✫ ✫ ✫

Thirteen charms on a silver band,
United hold our world in hand . . .
One and all, beware the day
Charms and bracelet break away.
Together they must always stay!

✫ ✫

The Silversmith clearly remembers Charm's coronation, when she presented the new queen with her bracelet. Charm knew she held the charms in trust, for the benefit of her people. Trust. Such a small word, thinks the Silversmith, but those who are trusted carry big responsibilities! She recalls

* *
✫Mede – month

4

how Zorgan, the wicked magician, very nearly destroyed Charm's trust in Sesame. She shakes her head at the thought of it and her long, silvery hair falls loosely around her shoulders.

"Thank the stars he didn't succeed!" she exclaims. "Thank goodness Charm knows that one day Sesame will return the lost charms, when she has found them all. Until then, they are safe with her in the Outworld."*

But how safe is her Seeker? Zorgan is in league with the queen's sister, Morbrecia, and his plan to snatch Sesame's locket and put her under a spell, to bring *him* the charms is unthinkable! If only she could find a way to warn Sesame . . .

The Silversmith glances at the thirteen magic candles; five still burn – glowing beacons of hope for their missing charms – and she hopes Sesame will return soon. So far the Charmseekers have outwitted Zorgan and Morbrecia, and Sesame has eight silver charms in her safekeeping.

* *
* Outworld – the name Karismans call our world

Turning to the window,
the Silversmith is amazed to see
a shooting star streaking across the
pale morning sky and, trailing in its wake,
a cascade of sparkling lights.

She sighs. It is a good sign . . .

Two

"How much more can you fit in there?" exclaimed Nic Brown. "It's only a *small* tent."

Sesame squeezed past her dad through the kitchen door, followed by her best friend, Maddy Webb. Each carried armfuls of rugs, sleeping bags, pillows, books, MP3s and teddies.

"Don't worry, Dad," said Sesame, skilfully balancing Alfie on top of her pile. "We'll manage."

"Mm," came Maddy's muffled voice from behind a pillow. "You need loads of stuff for camping, Mr Brown."

Nic shook his head in amusement and watched the girls stagger down the garden path, past the flower beds full of pink and yellow snapdragons, fragrant sweet peas and bright, red poppies to the grassy patch by the apple tree where they'd pitched the tent. It was a warm Saturday afternoon in early summer and he'd agreed Sesame and Maddy could camp overnight.

He was taking Jodie Luck to a glittering awards ceremony in town, but he'd arranged for Sesame's gran, Lossy, to keep an eye on Sesame and Maddy. Leaving the girls to organise themselves, he texted Jodie:

Looking forward to seeing you later. Meet here about 7pm? Nic x

I'll be there. Jodie xx ☺

Sesame lifted the flap and found Chips and Pins already inside the tent. Her inquisitive, mischievous cats couldn't resist exploring.

As soon as she'd unrolled her sleeping-bag Chips settled himself, purring contentedly. Sesame laughed.

"So, you're camping too!" she said.

Maddy gave a shout.

"Ouch!"

Pins had pounced on her wiggling toes. Like Sesame, Maddy was wearing shorts and a T-shirt and had been padding around in bare feet. She caught Pins and gave him a cuddle.

"I can't wait for our midnight feast," she said. She produced a bag of jellybeans and offered Sesame some.

"Mm, thanks," said Sesame, taking a handful. "We can tell scary stories in the dark."

"We'll need a torch for spooky faces," said Maddy. She rummaged through her belongings. "Oh, I've forgotten mine."

"I've got one somewhere," said Sesame. "Gran bought me a brill Star-Brite wand torch that glows in the dark. Come on. Race you to the house."

At seven o'clock, Sesame and Maddy were in the kitchen with Lossy, preparing snacks for their midnight feast. Suddenly, Nic appeared in the doorway looking flustered. He was wearing a smart, black dinner jacket with a white shirt, but from his collar dangled a loose bow tie.

"I can't tie this stupid thing," he grumbled. "Not used to dressing up. A lot of fuss if you ask me."

Lossy wiped her hands on her apron and came to his rescue.

"Here, let me do it," she said.

Fascinated, Sesame and Maddy watched her loop the shaped ends of the bow tie over, under, across and through each other, until she'd tied them perfectly. Nic turned to the girls for approval.

"There. How do I look?"

"Cooool!" they drawled.

"You look great, Dad," added Sesame. "Hope you win tonight."

"Win what?" asked Maddy.

Nic looked embarrassed.

"Oh, some award I've been nominated for," he muttered.

"*Some* award!" exploded Sesame. "Er, I think you mean The Daily Times Photojournalist of the Year Award."

"Wow!" said Maddy.

Nic blushed, checked his watch, then patted his pocket.

"Oops, nearly forgot the invitations," he said. "Where *did* I put them?"

Sesame rolled her eyes.

"Here, Dad," she said, handing him two gilt-edged cards from a shelf-tidy, crammed with bills and papers.

Seconds later, the doorbell rang.

"That'll be Jodie," said Nic, and he hurried away to greet her.

The girls gasped with delight when they saw Jodie. Their riding teacher was looking very glamorous in a long, silky, peach dress and high-heeled silver sandals. In one hand she clutched a beaded evening bag, and her earrings sparkled like stars. Nic thought she looked stunning.

"I *love* your dress," said Sesame.

"Gorgeous bag," added Maddy.

"You look lovely," said Lossy, echoing everyone's thoughts.

"Thank you," said Jodie shyly. She turned to Sesame and Maddy. "I hear you two are camping tonight. What fun!"

Nic glanced at his watch again.

"Time to go."

Lossy and the girls went to the car, to see them off.

"Good luck!" everyone chorused, as Nic and Jodie drove away.

Shortly afterwards, Sesame and Maddy made their way to the tent. It was a clear, starry night and the moon was full. Sesame had found her torch, but she didn't switch it on – the garden was flooded with moonlight. They heard Lossy call to them from the back door:

"I'll be down soon to say goodnight, girls."

Sesame waved and Lossy went inside. She switched on the television and settled down to watch the news.

Meanwhile, the girls were crossing the lawn when Sesame's necklace began to tingle. She'd felt this tingling sensation many times before, as though her special locket was trying to tell her something. Goose pimples pricked the nape of her neck and her tummy fluttered with excitement. What could it mean this time?

Something made her look up and she stopped dead in her tracks. Maddy crashed into her. She'd been carrying a plate of sandwiches and midnight treats which went flying.

"Ses," she protested. "You might've warned me—"

"Look," said Sesame. "A shooting star!"

"Wicked!" Maddy exclaimed.

They gawped in wonder at the meteor, which was sprinkling a trail of tiny stars across the heavens. Without warning, they found themselves caught up in the whirl of its glittering, golden light, twirling them faster and faster until Sesame felt her feet leave the ground.

"Help!" she cried, flinging out her arms to steady herself.

"Wait for me!" yelled Maddy.

Just in time she grabbed Sesame's foot and held on tight. Together they rocketed skywards, scarcely able to breathe they were going so fast. It was like zooming up in a lift – fifty floors without stopping – hurtling through time and space, in the wake of the star. Without a doubt, the Charmseekers knew they were on their way to the magical world of Karisma.

Three

Sesame and Maddy travelled from darkness to daylight in no time. Soon they were descending through a cascade of gold pinpricks of light, until they landed *Thump! Bump!* on a sandy beach. Sesame shook herself, amazed to find she was still holding her torch. She put it in the pocket of her shorts and looked about. Maddy lay sprawled nearby. She moaned as she got to her feet.

"Ow," she said, rubbing her knee. "Where are we?"

"Not sure . . ." said Sesame slowly. "It looks a *bit* like Butterfly Bay but—" She could see a headland jutting into the sea and beyond that, a distant shore. "I think we're on an island."

They were still wondering where they were when a blast of wind got up, so fierce it nearly blew them over. A spinning, spiralling golden cloud whirled from the sand, and from it emerged the figure of a woman.

She had a shawl of bright green seaweed fronds draped about her shoulders, her tangled hair was plaited with seashells.

"Fairday,* Charmseekers. I'm Ramora, Gatekeeper Nine. Welcome to Star Island!"

* *
*Fairday – a typical Karisman friendly greeting

18

For a few seconds the girls stared at her in stunned amazement, before Sesame managed to say:

"Hi! I'm— "

"Sesame Brown," said Ramora. "I know all about you and your friend, Maddy Webb. It's all in the weeds. I read them, you see."

Maddy looked puzzled.

"Weeds?"

"I'll show you," said Ramora. "Come in."

"In where?" asked Sesame. She couldn't see a building anywhere.

Ramora clapped her hands. There was a

BANG! A mini sand storm, then **POOF!**

A wooden hut appeared.

"My place," said Ramora.

"Um, excuse me," said Sesame, following Ramora into her hut. "Are you a . . . witch?"

"Not *a* witch," replied Ramora indignantly. "A *sand* witch."

Maddy started to giggle. The vision of a sandwich on a broomstick entered her head, but she didn't think Ramora would find it funny. She swallowed hard to control herself and followed Sesame inside.

Together they stepped into a cosy sitting room lit by lamps with pearly lampshades. A driftwood fire burned brightly in the fireplace. The room was crammed with curious things;

pots, bowls, trinkets and knick-knacks littered every shelf and table; on the walls were sea charts, star maps and pictures. A picture of the thirteen magical charms immediately caught Sesame's eye.

She pointed out five of them to the gatekeeper.

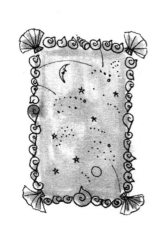

"The moon, star, dolphin, cloverleaf and key are still missing," she explained. "We've come to look for them. Sesame Brown will track them down!"

"We've found all the others," said Maddy.

"Yes, I know," said Ramora, with a smile. "The weeds, remember?" She took a clump of fresh seaweed from a jar and spread the strands on a tray. "They tell tales, if you know how to read them."

"Can we have a go?" asked Maddy.

"Please do," said Ramora.

Maddy and Sesame studied the seaweed for a short while. Maddy gave up, disappointed because she couldn't see a thing. But Sesame thought she'd spotted something.

"Look," she said, "A little star!"

"You have the gift of a Seeker," Ramora murmured. "The charm must be here somewhere . . . *so*, keep your eyes and ears open. The sooner you find *all* the charms the better! That evil magician Zorgan is after them." Catching sight of Sesame's necklace, she added: "He wants your pretty locket too."

Ramora had only confirmed what Sesame already knew, but hearing the sand witch say it sent shivers down her spine.

"Why *does* Zorgan want my locket?" she asked.

"Ah," said Ramora, pausing to choose her words carefully. Although she didn't want to scare Sesame, she had to warn her about the magician. "Zorgan needs a precious belonging, something you treasure. Once he has it he can cast a spell on you. Under his spell, you'd be forced to bring him the charms, even the ones you hold in the Outworld."

"Oh, Ses!" cried Maddy.

Although it was worse than she'd feared, Sesame wasn't put off. In fact, she felt more determined than ever to complete her quest.

"Don't worry," she said. "There's no way I'd give Zorgan the charms. They belong to Queen Charm!"

Ramora chuckled.

"That's the spirit," she said, and peered into her seaweed. Something she saw in the weeds made her frown. "Hushish!"* she exclaimed. "Bad sign. I see the letter 'M'."

Sesame and Maddy looked at each other.

"Morbrecia!" they groaned.

"I'm afraid so," said Ramora. "She'll make trouble for you. Morbrecia and Zorgan – they're in this together."

"Let's go, Maddy," said Sesame. "We must find the charm before Morbrecia does."

When they were all standing outside the hut, Maddy remembered about the gate.

"What time do we have to be back?" she asked Ramora.

* *
*Hushish – a word used to express dismay

"Look for my chimney," said the gatekeeper. "Six puffs of smoke and the gate shuts."

Then she went inside and closed the door.

Four

Morbrecia's favourite magical doll, Elmo, sat watching Morbrecia stick pins into Sesame's shoe! How fortunate for Sesame, thought Elmo, that she isn't wearing it! Not that it mattered. Sesame would soon feel the power of the pins, wherever she was . . .

The item of footwear under attack was a flip-flop – the one Sesame had lost on Agapogo Day a few medes ago. Morbrecia recalled she'd been chasing Sesame Brown and Maddy Webb through the streets of Lantern Hill. Sesame had found the beautiful silver shell and Morbrecia had *so* nearly snatched it from her. She jabbed yet another pin into the sandal and turned to Elmo.

26

"Sesame escaped and all I got was her shoe!" she said bitterly. "So far she's been lucky. She's got away with eight charms. But next time I'll be ready for her—"

Morbrecia stopped. Elmo's lips had started to move and suddenly words came tumbling from her mouth. Morbrecia knew they were not Elmo's words, not her voice. She'd know that voice anywhere. Zorgan! He used Elmo as a way to communicate with Morbrecia, so they could plot and plan together.

"Put aside the Seeker's shoe,
There's more important work to do.
Star Island is the place to be,
To lie in wait for - S-e-s-a-m-e!"

"I'll go to Star Island at once," said Morbrecia eagerly, although she grimaced at the idea of a boat trip. She felt seasick just thinking about it.

Five

The Charmseekers struck out along the bay and climbed the headland Sesame had seen earlier. From here they could see the whole of Star Island; it was shaped like a five pointed star. When they looked across the turquoise sea towards the mainland of Karisma, they picked out the familiar shape of Morbrecia's castle. With a sinking feeling, they realised it wasn't far away.

28

"I hope Morbrecia hasn't spotted us," said Maddy anxiously.

Sesame hoped so too. If the star charm *was* here, they'd have to work fast, before she caught up with them. But where should they begin? Sesame fingered her locket, trying to decide, but she couldn't get Ramora's warning about Zorgan out of her head. Forewarned, she'd have to take extra care of her locket from now on. Suddenly she  felt it tingle as she looked towards a long, sandy beach bordered by cliffs, and she was sure this was a sign.

"Come on," she said to Maddy. "We'll start there."

The tide was out. Sesame and Maddy walked barefoot along a stretch of golden sand, peering into rock pools and under stones, hoping to catch a tell tale glint of silver. Splashing through a shallow pool, Sesame felt a sharp pain in her left foot. It was quickly followed by another and another. It was like pins and needles, only worse.

"Ouch!" she yelped, hopping on one leg.

"What's up, Ses?" said Maddy.

"I must have trodden on something," said Sesame.

They hunted round for a sharp object, but there was nothing there. Sesame gave her sore foot a rub.

"Weird," she said. And thought no more of it.

Some time later, as they rounded a craggy cliff, they were surprised to see footprints in the sand. Large, webbed footprints . . . and lots of them.

"I wonder who they belong to?" said Sesame, scanning the beach. She couldn't see anyone about.

"Big ducks?" joked Maddy.

"Ssh!" said Sesame. "Listen."

It was the unmistakable sound of voices singing:

"Pebbles, shells, glass and wood,
Shiny metal findings.
We're the folk who pick them up –
The lost and left-behindings!"

When the singers came marching out from behind a big rock, Sesame and Maddy found themselves gawping at five skinny boys. They had slime-green bodies and flat, webbed feet and each carried a bulging sack.

The boys stopped singing and looked very alarmed to see strangers on their beach. The biggest took a step forward and eyed the girls suspiciously.

"Who are you?" he said.

"I'm Sesame," said Sesame. "This is my friend Maddy. Who are *you*?"

"Tyke," said Tyke. "We're Urchins."* He jabbed a thumb at his companions. "My chinners."**

His friends called out their names:

"I'm Gumba! Lumsy! Lug! Fiz!"

"Do you live on Star Island?" asked Maddy.

Tyke shuffled his webbed feet and avoided answering her question.

"We're . . . *staying* here," he said.

"We're from The Swamps," said Gumba, with a nod towards the mainland.

"I think we've been there!" said Sesame. She remembered the time she, Maddy, Gemma and Liz had come to Karisma in a magic bubble. They'd landed in a marshy place and had to squelch through the mud in their slippers. Maybe *that's* why urchins have webbed feet, she thought.

"How did you get here?" Maddy asked.

"We were fishing off rocks near Butterfly Bay," said Lumsy. He looked embarrassed: "Got cut off by the tide . . ."

"Clung to some driftwood," added Lug, "and landed here."

* *
* **Urchins** – web-footed people of The Swamps
** **Chinners** – Urchin slang, meaning 'mates'

32

The smallest urchin called Fiz began to sniffle.

"I want to go home," he said.

"Well, you can't," shouted Tyke. "We're stuck!"

There was an awkward silence. Sesame and Maddy felt especially sorry for Fiz, but they couldn't see how they could help. Maddy tried to make conversation.

"We're Charmseekers—" she began.

"Charm-s-e-e-k-e-r-s," drawled Tyke. "You're looking for charms?"

"You won't find anything here," said Gumba. "It's boring. We've found all there is to find."

"Anyway this is *our* beach now," said Lumsy defensively. "Everything belongs to us."

"They're our left-behindings," said Lug.

"Left-behindings?" queried Maddy.

Tyke rattled the contents of his sack.

"Ah," said Sesame, cottoning on. She remembered their song: 'Pebbles, shells, glass and wood, shiny metal findings . . .' "You *collect* things!" As she said it, an idea whizzed into her head. Perhaps the urchins could help them look for the charm? There was a chance they'd already found it. She was wondering how best to ask them, when Maddy blurted out:

"We collect charms!"

Sesame rolled her eyes at Maddy. The urchins – all except Fiz – didn't look too happy. Fiz thought the girls seemed friendly, so he smiled at them shyly.

"Um, not exactly," said Sesame, thinking fast. "We're searching for some lost charms so we can give them back to Queen Charm."

"One of them *might* be on the island," said Maddy. "A silver star. Have you seen it?"

"No!" said Lumsy, a little too quickly.

Fiz shot him a look.

"Lumsy—" he began.

But the other urchins glared at him and Fiz

 cowered, afraid to say more. Sesame felt sure they knew *something* about the charm and the thought of them not telling her made her mad.

Losing your temper isn't going to help, she told herself. Keep your cool, Sesame. Try and gain their trust . . .

"*Please* help us," she said. "It's really important we find the charms. They're magic. I don't know how, but they help nature, the weather, the climate – *everything*. Since they were stolen from the queen, terrible things have been happening. The winds have changed, butterflies can't migrate, the ice is melting, crops have been ruined . . . oh, loads of stuff!"

"Yes," said Maddy. "And things will go on getting worse, until all the charms are found."

"Is that why we got cut off by the tide?" asked Fiz timidly. "Was it because the magic charms were lost?"

His four friends sniggered. To the girls' dismay, none of what they'd said seemed to have had the slightest effect on *them*. Tyke folded his arms and scowled at Sesame.

"Why should we believe you?" he said. "I bet you're making it up. Nothing bad's happened here. We're jammo." *

"You just want our left-behindings," said Gumba.

"We *might* know where the charm is . . ." teased Lumsy.

* *
* **Jammo** – Urchin slang for good or okay

35

"Even if we did, we wouldn't tell you!" said Lug.

And they ran off singing, tugging a reluctant Fiz along with them.

**"Pebbles, shells, glass
and wood, shiny metal findings.
We're the folk who pick them up
- the lost and left- behindings!"**

Six

"Stop rocking the boat," yelled Morbrecia. "I feel sick!"

After Zorgan's tip about Sesame's whereabouts, Morbrecia had hastily picked four footmen and ordered them to sail her to Star Island. A brisk breeze whipped up the waves. The footmen did their best to handle the billowing sails, but it seemed the wind was blowing them on a course of its own. And her crew had never sailed before. Miserably, Morbrecia hung over the side, her face an astonishing shade of green. And still the sea swelled up and down, up and down . . .

At last, they reached Star Island. The crew anchored off a sandy cove and Morbrecia 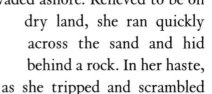 waded ashore. Relieved to be on dry land, she ran quickly across the sand and hid behind a rock. In her haste, as she tripped and scrambled over the hot sand, a silver buckle flew off her shoe.

"Blatz!"✷ she cursed. She could see the buckle lying a little way away, but she didn't want to be seen. "I'll fetch it later," she said.

She scanned the beach. To her right was a maze of rocks and to her left, five small caves at the foot of a cliff. She could see no sign of Sesame. Was the Charmseeker alone or with friends? Zorgan hadn't said. She wished she could look into his crystal ball and see what was going on . . .

✷ ✷
✷ **Blatz** – a really angry exclamation

Zorgan, meanwhile, had been keeping his eye on Sesame and Maddy. Ever since they'd arrived on Star Island, he'd observed their every move through his crystal ball. He'd even glimpsed inside Ramora's hut, while she was reading her seaweed. He'd been very surprised to learn the gatekeeper knew of his plans to put a spell on Sesame . . .

"Interfering witch and her weeds!" he fumed. "Ramora knows too much for her own good. But I *will* have Sesame's locket. She *will* bring me the charms!"

From his Star Room, Zorgan looked across to the island. He prided himself on having taken control of Morbrecia's boat, setting it on course for one particular beach. He smiled, as he stroked his pet bandrall,✶ Vanda.

"My windy spell did the trick," he told her with

* *
✶ **Bandrall** – rare flying mammal, native to Karisma

smug satisfaction. "Now it's up to Morbrecia. She must deal with Sesame Brown!"

"One of them must have found the charm," said Sesame crossly. "I *know* it."

Maddy agreed.

"It was the way they looked at each other," she said. "I wonder who?"

"Even if we knew," said Sesame, "how would we persuade him to give it up? I bet if Fiz had found the star he'd have said, but he's afraid of the others. They're SO mean to him."

"Mm," commiserated Maddy. "And they don't care about what's happening in Karisma. Just because they're okay, they think nothing else matters. They can't be bothered to help."

"I reckon they're just bored," said Sesame. "They're collecting 'lost and left-behindings' because there's nothing else to do."

"In a way that's good, isn't it?" said Maddy.

"Yes, it's brill," agreed Sesame. "The urchins don't know it, but they're helping the environment!"

"I wonder what they're going to do with all that stuff?" said Maddy. "I haven't noticed any recycling banks here."

Sesame grinned.

"Well, maybe they could start one!" she said.

They'd been following the urchins' footprints through a maze of rocks and had come to a sandy cove. Anchored a little way off shore they saw a sailing boat.

"I wonder who that belongs to?" said Maddy. "I can't see anyone about."

The girls were still puzzling over the boat and where the urchins could have gone, when they spotted the five caves.

"I reckon they're hiding in there," said Sesame.

"And one of them has the charm!" said Maddy.

She felt so cross and frustrated with the urchins that she walked round in circles, kicking at the sand. Sesame leaned against a rock to think.

"The urchins are a problem," she said, "but we've faced more difficult challenges than them. Remember the gribblers ✷ and the skreels?" ✷✷

✷ **Gribbler** – extremely unpleasant goblin-like creature with yellow teeth and bad breath

✷✷ **Skreel** – small flesh-eating fish

Maddy nodded and came over.

"And Zorgan's pixies, Nix and Dina," she said.

"Not forgetting the drakons!"* added Sesame.

"So what now?" said Maddy. "We haven't got time to play stupid guessing games with the urchins. It won't be long before the gate closes."

"I know," said Sesame. "But we can't give up. Anyway I've just thought of a brilliant plan . . ."

* *
*Drakon — large fire-breathing insect

Seven

"We're going to trick them into *showing* us!" said Sesame.

"R-i-g-h-t," said Maddy.

Sesame explained.

"Look, we know they pick things up from the beach," she said. "Remember their song? Well, supposing they each collect one type of thing. Fiz was about to tell us before the others shut him up. Maybe Tyke likes pebbles; Gumba, shells; Fiz, glass . . . get it? That means one of them collects *shiny metal*—"

"Cool!" said Maddy. "So one of them'll have the charm. But I don't see how they're going to show us. "

"You soon will," said Sesame. "Listen. Here's what we'll do . . ."

When she'd finished, they gave each other their secret Charmseekers hand sign, for luck.

44

Meanwhile, from her hiding place behind a craggy rock, Morbrecia had a perfect view of the girls. At first, it seemed the pair were busily occupied looking for the charms. Morbrecia chuckled to herself. With any luck those interfering Charmseekers will find a charm, she thought. And I'll be waiting to grab it! However, after a while, Morbrecia had the feeling something wasn't quite right. She was baffled. What *were* they up to?

"Ooo! Here's a pretty shell," exclaimed Sesame, in a loud voice. She was holding up an empty shell, pearly-pink with bright red stripes.

"Look, Ses," cried Maddy. "I've found some driftwood and a pebble!"

They were shouting on purpose, hoping to attract the urchins' attention. It was all part of Sesame's plan. After they'd been searching for a bit longer, Maddy said out of the corner of her mouth:

"Supposing we don't find any glass and metal things?"

"We must," said Sesame. "My idea won't work without them."

They both knew time was slipping by. They'd been keeping an eye on Ramora's hut on the far side of the cove; the last time Maddy checked, she'd counted three puffs of smoke from the chimney.

Maddy suddenly let out an excited squeal. She'd spotted a broken necklace of glass beads, washed up on the shore. She held it up, hoping the urchins might see. A few minutes later, Sesame chanced upon something silver, glinting in the sand. Her tummy flipped and, for a thrilling moment, she thought she'd found a charm. To her disappointment, she discovered it was only a shiny shoe buckle.

"You should be pleased," said Maddy. "Now we can set the trap!"

The girls strolled near the caves, casually dropping the shell, pebble, driftwood, necklace and buckle as they went along.

Sesame and Maddy wandered about, as if they had all the time in the world to enjoy themselves. Sesame dramatically wiped her hand across her forehead.

"Phew! I'm really hot," she shouted. "Let's go for a swim!"

"Good idea," cried Maddy. "The sea looks lovely."

But instead of swimming, they hid behind some rocks and watched to see what would happen. They didn't have to wait long. The urchins couldn't resist the 'left-behindings'. They came scuttling out of their caves and each put something in his sack . . .

Can you see what each urchin put in his sack? Remember, only one of them collects shiny metal things, so who is most likely to have the charm? Is it Tyke, Gumba, Lumsy, Lug or Fiz?

Sesame's plan was working! First came Tyke . . .
then Gumba . . . Lug was next . . . followed by Fiz .
. . And last of all came Lumsy, who picked up the
shiny silver buckle! He was about to put it in his
sack, when Sesame and Maddy sprang from their
hiding place.

"You're the one with the charm!" accused Sesame.

"Open your sack," demanded Maddy.

Taken by surprise, Lumsy dropped the buckle.
But he soon recovered.

"What if I have?" he sneered. "What are you
going to do about it?"

Sesame was ready. She smiled sweetly at him.

"Swap you for it?" she said.

"Swap what?" said Lumsy.

His friends crowded round,
curious to see what Sesame
had to offer.

"This," she said, suddenly
producing her torch. "My glow-
in-the-dark Star-Brite wand torch!
Guaranteed waterproof and shockproof."
She switched it on and off, for dramatic
effect.

The urchins were awestruck. They
thought the torch was amazing.

"A light stick!" said Tyke, taking a step
closer.

50

"It must be magic," said Gumba.

"Mm," said Maddy, trying to keep a straight face.

"You can use it in emergencies," added Sesame.

She switched her Star-Brite wand torch to signal mode and set off a flashing beacon.

"Done!" cried Lumsy.

He grabbed the torch, then shook the contents from his sack.
A jumbled assortment of tins, a rusty bucket, a bent spoon, a broken watch, a length of chain, an iron ring and some coins came spilling out. Frantically, Sesame and Maddy sorted through the junk, but they couldn't see the charm.

"Where is it?" cried Sesame, afraid the urchin had tricked her.

"I-I-haven't got it," said Lumsy, snatching up his sack. "Fooled you though, didn't I!"

"Give it to me," said Sesame. making a grab for the sack. "I want to see for myself."

But Lumsy was too quick and backed away.

"You'll have to catch me first," he said.

"Oh, Lumsy!" cried Fiz. "That's not fair."

The other urchins rounded on him, but this time he stood up to them.

"I think we should help the Charmseekers," said Fiz, sounding much bolder than he felt. "It's important they find all the magical charms 'cos they help everything and I know you've got the star Lumsy 'cos I saw you pick it up!"

Lumsy was furious. He made to give Fiz a cuff round the ear, but Tyke stopped him. He'd been thinking. What if the star charm was magic, as Sesame had said it was. If they kept it, would it bring them bad luck? Tyke took charge of the situation.

"Open the sack," he ordered Lumsy.

"Wha—" began Lumsy.

"Just do it," said Tyke.

Lumsy didn't dare argue with Tyke. Moodily he opened his sack and gave it another shake and . . .

out flew the little star! It was perfect. The silver charm twinkled and shone with a shimmering light of its own – as bright as any star in the sky.

Eight

Sesame and Maddy were never quite sure what happened next. Everything whizzed by in a blur. All they could remember was Morbrecia appearing from nowhere to snatch the charm.

It was the moment the princess had been waiting for. Lurking behind her rock, watching and listening, she'd timed her attack perfectly. The second after Morbrecia saw the star fall from Lumsy's sack, she sprang into action. She raced from her hiding place, her jet-black hair streaming in the wind.

"Mine!" she screeched, as she swooped on the charm.

Instinctively, Sesame dived for the star. Maddy made a grab for Morbrecia's shoe — the one without the buckle — and it slipped off her foot.

Morbrecia aimed a swift kick at Maddy, and missed. Sesame, meanwhile, was fiercely struggling to release the charm from Morbrecia's clamped fist.

"LET GO!" she cried, but as she fought, her locket got caught in Morbrecia's hair.

"Ow!" yelped Morbrecia, using her free hand to wrench the locket from her locks. She used *such* force that – *SNAP!* The chain broke. Seizing her chance, Morbrecia snatched the locket from Sesame's neck and held it up triumphantly.

"Oh!" wailed Sesame.

"No!" shouted Maddy.

"Vixee!"* exclaimed Morbrecia. "A charm *and* your locket, Sesame Brown. You're in BIG trouble now!"

Sesame lunged at her, but Morbrecia was too quick. She ran, one shoe on and the other off, with Sesame and Maddy pelting after her.

* * * * * * * * * * * * * * * *

* **Vixee** – a gleeful, triumphant exclamation meaning great or wicked

During this time, the urchins had been oblivious to everything going on around them – all except Fiz, who had stood aside, watching with a bewildered expression on his face. He was too little to help Sesame and Maddy wrestle the charm from Morbrecia and, to make matters worse, a fight had broken out between the urchins.

After Lumsy had taken possession of Sesame's torch, Tyke, Gumba and Lug quarrelled over it. First Tyke snatched it from Lumsy, then Gumba grabbed it from Tyke, who was jumped on by Lug. By the time they'd all stopped fighting and had agreed to share the torch, Sesame and Maddy were nowhere in sight. But Fiz had watched them go . . .

★ ⋆ ★

Zorgan could barely contain his excitement. He'd been following Morbrecia's progress in his crystal ball, and had seen her swoop on the charm *and* snatch Sesame's locket.

"Spallah!"* he exclaimed. "I shall soon have Sesame under my spell."

He was also aware that time was running out for the Charmseekers to return to the gate. Zorgan crossed the room to look through his powerful

* *
* Spallah – excellent! A triumphant expression

55

telescope. He swivelled the eyepiece and focused it on the gatekeeper's hut. Between the hut and the cove was a rocky bay. Sesame mustn't get away. Somehow he must cut off her escape . . .

The magician opened his Book of Tried and Trusted Sea Spells and leafed through the pages, until he found one that sounded just right. For maximum effect, the spell required him to drink some salty water, before chanting the words.

Nix and Dina were standing by. Zorgan turned to the pixies, barking orders.

"Bring me water, a large goblet and some salt," he commanded.

Immediately the pixies flew off to carry out their tasks. Nix returned first, struggling with the biggest goblet she could find. Then came Dina with a jug of water and a pot of salt.

Zorgan poured the water into the goblet, added the salt and swirled it around. He held his nose, took a sip and . . . SPAT IT OUT. It tasted foul!

He was sure the spell would work anyway, so he tipped the salty drink away and intoned:

> *"Ebb and flow, come and go,*
> *Waves high, waters low.*
> *Tide turn, oh, salty sea –*
> *Seal the fate of S-e-s-a-m-e!"*

Back on the beach Sesame and Maddy were gaining on Morbrecia. Hampered by losing her shoe, Morbrecia couldn't run as quickly as the girls. Cursing Maddy, she splashed through a rock pool and didn't see the crab . . .

It was huge – a giant of a beast – waving two enormous pincers and lying in wait for its prey. When Morbrecia's bare foot landed right in front of it –

SNAP!

The crab clamped her toe in one colossal claw.

"OWWOOO!"

screamed Morbrecia, letting fly Sesame's locket and the charm in one go.

The Charmseekers couldn't believe their luck. The locket went sailing through the air and Maddy, who was a few steps ahead of Sesame, caught it neatly. Morbrecia looked daggers at Maddy, but there was nothing she could do. The crab clung on tight and she couldn't move. The star charm spiralled and fell *smack* into the crab's other claw!

"This is so not fair!" wailed Sesame, in frustration. One second the charm had been flying free. Then it wasn't.

But what happened next took them all by surprise. The tide turned without warning and, with a thunderous roar, a terrifying wall of water rose from the sea. Morbrecia and the girls stared in horror. It was the biggest wave they had ever seen – and it was heading straight for them!

Nine

Morbrecia was terrified. She screamed at her footmen in the boat; they had been lying on deck having a nap.

"Don't just sit there, magworts.* Help me!"

Maddy looked panic-stricken and wanted to run. Sesame was scared stiff too. She glanced at the wall of water thundering towards them. In a few minutes, she reckoned, it would swamp them. Out of the corner of her eye, she spotted five small boys pelting towards them, carrying their sacks of left-behindings. The urchins had seen the wave coming and hoped the Charmseekers could help. Fiz was leading the way, waving Sesame's torch. It was flashing a bright orange signal . . .

Meanwhile, Sesame's thoughts were racing.

"We can't leave Morbrecia," she shouted to Maddy. "She'll drown! And there's the charm—"

* *

* **Magwort** — probably the worst name you could call anyone! General term for a fool

Without another thought, Sesame tried to prize the giant claw open, to free Morbrecia's foot. Morbrecia looked at Sesame. She could scarcely believe what was happening.

"Why—?" she began then yelped with pain. "Ouch! That hurt. Watch what you're doing!"

Taking no notice, Sesame strained with all her strength, until suddenly the claw snapped open, and Morbrecia was free. Cursing the crab and without a backwards glance, she limped away to her boat.

The crab fixed Sesame with two, tiny black eyes. In a split-second, there passed between them some kind of mutual trust and understanding. Somehow the crab knew Sesame had come to help, knew she should have care of the charm. And with a *click!* she released the star.

"At last!" said Sesame, clasping it in her hand. Next instant, she and Maddy were swept off the rocks, along with the five urchins – everyone buoyed along on the crest of a foaming wave. Maddy screamed and grabbed Sesame's hand.

"Wha-what's happening?" she yelled.

They were all skimming along on the wave like surfers and going so fast it took their breath away.

"Weeeeee!"

shouted Tyke, Gumba, Lumsy, Lug and Fiz. It was all they could do to hold on to their sacks.

"Look!" shouted Sesame, pointing ahead. She could see Ramora's hut and puffs of smoke from the chimney. "The wave is taking us to the gate!"

The sand witch was waiting for them as the wave gently dumped the girls at her feet. Ramora clapped her hands and shooed it back to sea.

"Take the urchins safely home," Ramora whispered to the wave, then she added with a mysterious smile, "Thank you."

After the urchins had waved and shouted their goodbyes and thank you's to the Charmseekers, Sesame turned to Ramora.

"We've got the charm," she said. Proudly, she showed the gatekeeper the little star.

"Morbrecia nearly got away with Sesame's locket!" gasped Maddy. She was still holding tight to the broken chain.

"I know," said Ramora. "I saw it in the weeds. I hope Morbrecia appreciates your kindness, Sesame, though I doubt it! Now hurry, Charmseekers. The gate is closing. Setfair.* Come back soon!"

* *
* Setfair — goodbye and good luck

Sesame and Maddy ran into a gold and silvery, slightly gritty, mist that was rising from the sand. It spun them round, faster and faster, until they were spinning through the air, flying through the pink clouds of sunset, into the starry, night sky of home.

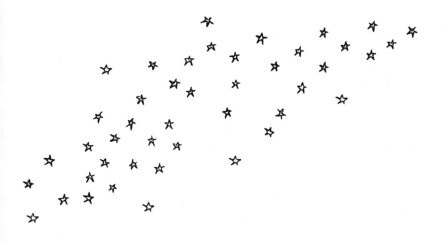

They drifted down on a beam of moonlight and landed on the lawn. Chips and Pins greeted them, purring. After their amazing adventure, the girls were in a daze and it took them a few minutes to recover. Everything was exactly as they'd left it – except for some tell tale grains of sand sprinkled on their sleeping bags.

Soon they heard Lossy calling their names, as she came down the garden path.

"Sleeping bags, quick!" whispered Sesame, groping around in the dark. "I wish I had my torch!"

"I wonder if those urchins have still got it," said Maddy, unzipping her bag.

When Lossy lifted the flap, a shaft of moonlight shone on the girls' smiling faces.

"Everything all right, campers?" she asked.

"We're fine, Gran," said Sesame happily.

"Yes," said Maddy. "Camping is cool."

"Good," said Lossy. "Don't stay up too late talking. I know what you two are like!"

"I hope Dad wins the award tonight," said Sesame, kissing her gran goodnight.

"I have a sneaking feeling he might," said Lossy.

And she went back to the house.

✴   ✫   ✫   ✫

Sesame had thought to slip her special jewellery box under her pillow. Now, by the light of the moon, she opened it. She and Maddy took it in turns to hold the silver star charm, turning it this way and that to admire the way it glistened, before Sesame carefully placed it with the others in the box. Seeing the nine beautiful charms together, remembering all they'd been through to find them, gave the girls a thrill.

"Gosh," said Maddy. "I hope we find the others before Zorgan and Morbrecia do." She gave a sleepy yawn. "D'you think we will, Ses?"

"We must," said Sesame, firmly closing the lid. "Whatever it takes . . ."

Sesame looked at her broken necklace. A little shiver ran down her spine, as she remembered how savagely Morbrecia had wrenched it from her. She'd come SO close to losing it! The locket, she knew, was easily mended. Keeping it safe from Zorgan was the problem.

The moon slipped behind a cloud, as Sesame zipped up the tent. Later, when Lossy peeped in to make sure all was well, she found the girls sound asleep.

Ten

The Silversmith claps her hands with joy. Sesame has the little star charm safe! The magic candle that bears its name has gone out. Now four candles remain alight – four charms yet to be found. She remembers each one so clearly; the crescent-moon, the cloverleaf, the key and the dolphin . . .

She knows the Charmseekers have put themselves at risk to save the star charm. And this time something happened to make her fear more than ever for her Seeker. She knew the instant Sesame had been parted from her locket. She'd felt the pain of it breaking. It was as if something had snapped inside her. For a while, she'd felt their bond broken, and had known that her Seeker was in grave danger of falling under Zorgan's spell. But all is well, she tells herself, for the time being at least . . .

The Silversmith knows she has chosen wisely in trusting Sesame to complete her quest. Her Seeker cares for her own world and for Karisma, too. She won't give up until she's found all the charms. Meanwhile, Karisma is in peril and nowhere has escaped the consequences of Zorgan's foolishness in scattering the charms. Neither on land, nor in the air, nor in the sea. Even in the depths of the ocean, things have been thrown out of balance and the mermaids and sea creatures are suffering . . . but that is another story. It must be told another day!